WINDOWS ON MAIN STREET

**Discover the Real Stories
of the Talented People
Featured on the Windows
of Main Street, U.S.A.**

CHUCK SNYDER

Disney
EDITIONS

NEW YORK

Foreword

Recently, I received a call from Jay Rasulo, chairman of the Parks and Resorts division of The Walt Disney Company. "We want to do a window for you on Main Street in *Disneyland* Park," Jay said. Wow! What a great honor! But I declined. It wasn't just that my name is already on the windows of Main Streets in Paris, Hong Kong, and Magic Kingdom Park in *Walt Disney World* Resort. It was because to add a *Disneyland* Park window for me now would be breaking the rules that I helped create and in many ways have championed. Who wouldn't want their name on a window in *Disneyland* Park, especially me? I began my fifty-plus-year Disney career at *Disneyland* Park in June 1955—one month before the Park opened.

But the rules state: aside from the names of the "original" Disney cast members who were responsible for designing, building, and enabling the creation of Disneyland Park, names of key cast members are added only upon their retirement.

This tradition was established by Walt Disney for *Disneyland* Park. He personally selected the names that would be revealed on the Main Street windows on Opening Day, July 17, 1955. With the exception of a few "outsiders" Walt chose to honor, that's the way it's been for more than half a century.

This unique public recognition, born at *Disneyland* Park, was continued by Walt's brother, Roy O. Disney, on Main Street in Magic Kingdom Park in Florida. In fact, Roy wrote me a note stating that he "wanted to do this exactly as Walt had in *Disneyland* Park." And he even wrote out an example, in which he misspelled my name (Marty Skalar!).

Obviously, the honor is high, and the windows are few. Therefore, an individual's achievements need to be of the very highest level to warrant inclusion with the originals who created and built a particular park. That is a subjective judgment, but it is always at the forefront of the decision to add a name to these very public, very visible positions of honor within our parks around the world.

So, to add a name today, there are three requirements:
1. Only on retirement.
2. Only the highest level of service/respect/achievement.
3. Agreement between top individual park management and Walt Disney Imagineering, which creates the design and copy concepts.

I am so happy that this illuminating book is being published. You can be sure that I'll be sending Jay Rasulo a note with this copy: "Please remember the rules (and me!) when I retire!"

Marty Sklar
Executive Vice President
Imagineering Ambassador

Introduction

It has often been said, and originally by Walt himself, that The Walt Disney Company was all started by a mouse. Perhaps it could be said, then, that the Disney Parks were all started by a polo injury. For it was after Walt injured his back playing polo in the 1930s that his doctor encouraged him to find a new hobby. Walt had a love of miniatures and railroads; thus his new hobby turned out to be miniature railroads. Walt immersed himself in his railroad hobby, working after hours in his studio's machine shop, where he eventually built his own miniature steam engine, the Lilly Belle. With this little steam engine, Walt's imagination and creativity were forever set free from the limitations of the two-dimensional world of the Disney animated movies, to roam in a new and exciting three-dimensional world.

On December 16, 1952, with his mind full of new ideas, Walt formed his own creative company, WED Enterprises (later renamed Walt Disney Imagineering), to develop plans for a family entertainment venue to be known as *Disneyland* Park. There would be no miniature train in this park; his interests and ideas had progressed to the point that everything would now be life-size. He wanted his park to be of the highest quality, like his motion pictures, and he hired only the best people to assist him. Some were already on his staff, working at his Burbank studio; others would be hired specifically for the project. But they all shared one characteristic: a belief in an idea that existed only in Walt's imagination and that had never been realized before.

Today, the idea to build *Disneyland* Park seems like an easy decision. At the time, however, the risks for all involved were great, and success was far from guaranteed. Fortunately, the crowds came on July 17, 1955, and they have continued to come ever since.

Walt Disney World Resort was risky in another way. Built partly on swampland, the "Florida Project" was, at the time, the largest privately funded construction project in the world, costing $400 million. The 1964–1965 New York World's Fair, which featured four Disney-created attractions, proved the viability of and interest in an East Coast park. Roy O. Disney, Walt's brother, who headed the project after Walt's death in 1966, built a vacation kingdom that is still the most visited resort destination in the world.

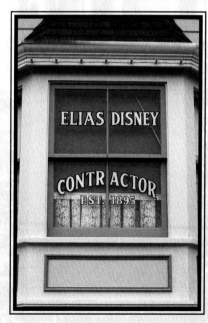

This book is about the men and women whose creative visions, tireless efforts, "can-do" attitudes, teamwork, and ability to dream have brought a smile to the face of anyone who has visited a Disney Park. The ultimate honor for these Cast Members, as employees are known, is to have their names emblazoned on a window in the Main Street, U.S.A. Area. To the typical park Guest, these names appear to be the calling cards of make-believe shopkeepers. In reality, the names belong to the "all-stars" of the parks' histories. As one walks around Main Street, U.S.A. Area, these names are the opening credits of a show like no other.

Following is an alphabetical sampling of some of these talented people and their accomplishments, as well as a complete list of all *Disneyland* Park and *Walt Disney World* Resort honorees. They are all responsible for bringing Walt's park ideas to fruition. And it only took faith and trust . . . and just a little bit of pixie dust.

KEN ANDERSON
Disneyland

Walt Disney referred to Ken Anderson as his "jack-of-all-trades." Already an artist at Walt's studio, and with a background in architecture, Ken was tapped by Walt to assist with the opening of *Disneyland* Park. He made many

contributions to Fantasyland Area, including Storybook Land Canal Boats, Snow White's Scary Adventures, Peter Pan's Flight, and Mr. Toad's Wild Ride. Later, he designed the Sleeping Beauty Castle dioramas and contributed concepts for The Haunted Mansion Attraction. Ken was an avid fly fisherman. The Bait Co. mention in his window was a backhanded gag written by Walt, who knew that fly fishermen do not use bait.

BUDDY BAKER
Walt Disney World

Buddy Baker began his Disney career in 1954, when his former student at Los Angeles City College, composer George Bruns, needed help arranging music for the TV show *Davy Crockett*. When Bruns grew tired of writing music for the Park, he gave the assignments to Buddy, who would go on to compose the music for The Haunted Mansion Attraction and write the orchestrations for "it's a small world," Walt Disney's Carousel of Progress, Great Moments with Mr. Lincoln, The Hall of Presidents, and If You Had Wings. Buddy came out of retirement to supervise the music for *Epcot*®, where he personally arranged the music for seven attractions: Universe of Energy, The American Adventure, World of Motion, Kitchen Kabaret, Listen to The Land, and the films *Wonders of China* and *Impressions de France*.

X ATENCIO *Disneyland and Walt Disney World*

X Atencio started his Disney career in 1938 as an animation in-betweener before transferring to WED in 1965, where Walt asked him to write the script for the Pirates of the Caribbean Attraction. A writing novice at the time, X also wrote the lyrics for the attraction's song, "Yo Ho (A Pirate's Life for Me)," teaming up with studio composer George Bruns. X's voice is used in the attraction as that of the talking skull and crossbones. He later wrote the script for The Haunted Mansion Attraction and its song, "Grim Grinning Ghosts," this time teaming with composer Buddy Baker. For *Walt Disney World* Resort, he contributed to Space Mountain and If You Had Wings in Magic Kingdom Park, and Spaceship Earth, World of Motion, and the Mexico pavilion in *Epcot*®.

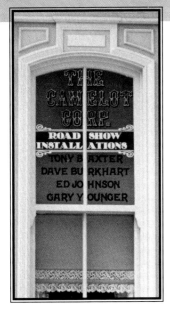

TONY BAXTER
Walt Disney World

Tony Baxter began his Disney career at *Disneyland* Park in 1965, where he was a sweeper, ice-cream scooper, and ride operator. He later became a WED model designer and was a member of the on-site *Walt Disney World* Resort design team for the resort's opening in 1971, where his involvement was on Snow White's Scary Adventures and 20,000 Leagues Under the Sea. An "idea guy," Tony is responsible for many great Disney theme park attraction concepts, including Big Thunder Mountain Railroad Attraction, Star Tours, Indiana Jones™ Adventure, Tarzan's Treehouse, and Splash Mountain, which he conceived while in a traffic jam on his way to *Disneyland* Park. He also was the show producer for the original Journey into Imagination in *Epcot*®. The Camelot Corp. heading in his window refers to Orlando's Camelot Apartments, where many California transplants lived while working on *Walt Disney World* Resort.

WALLY BOAG
Disneyland

The original Pecos Bill in the Golden Horseshoe Revue in *Disneyland* Park beginning in 1955, Wally Boag would go on to perform the show nearly 40,000 times. For his Golden Horseshoe Revue audition, Wally performed for Walt on June 14, 1955, on an empty soundstage at the Studio, after which he was given a two-week contract. He was later asked to voice the parrot, José, in The Enchanted Tiki Room Attraction, for which he also helped write the script. For *Walt Disney World* Resort, Wally was both producer and performer for the opening of the Diamond Horseshoe Revue in *Magic Kingdom* Park.

MARY BLAIR *Walt Disney World*

Mary Blair is best known as the designer and color stylist for the "it's a small world" Attraction. She was hired in 1940 as an artist in the story department, to add more stylistic visuals to the Studio's animated films, and Walt called on her to help out with "it's a small world" for the 1964–1965 New York World's Fair. For *Walt Disney World* Resort, Mary assisted with designing the Grand Canyon Concourse in Disney's Contemporary Resort, where she created the colorful nine-story-high tiled mural in which she jokingly included a five-legged goat.

CHUCK BOYAJIAN *Disneyland*

Although his *Disneyland* Park window states, "We Keep Your Castle Shining," Chuck Boyajian was known for keeping entire Disney parks sparkling clean. He was hired by Walt in 1955 as the first manager of Custodial Operations in *Disneyland* Park. Believing that "cleanliness breeds cleanliness," he strove to make Walt's vision of having the cleanest park in the world a reality. Chuck later assisted with the opening of *Walt Disney World* Resort. When a nervous new sweeper once asked for guidance, Chuck replied, "How spic do I want the area? Well, I'll tell you, son. No less than span!"

ROGER BROGGIE

Disneyland and Walt Disney World

Roger Broggie was hired by Walt in 1939 to maintain the camera equipment at the original Hyperion Avenue animation studio. Named head of the Studio's machine shop in 1950, he was recruited to WED in 1952 by Walt to head the development of ride, mechanical, and show systems for *Disneyland* Park. Audio-Animatronics, Circle-Vision 360 films, and the *Disneyland* Park monorail were all developed under Roger's leadership. For *Walt Disney World* Resort, he directed the design and construction of the *Walt Disney World* Railroad, the Skyway (since removed), WEDway Peoplemover (now the Tomorrowland Transit Authority), and the monorail. One of the trains of the *Walt Disney World* Railroad is named in his honor.

HARRIET BURNS *Disneyland*

Hired in 1955 to build sets and props for the *Mickey Mouse Club* television show, Harriet Burns later became the first female Imagineer, working in the model shop. There, she created the models that would later become full-size buildings and figures in *Disneyland* Park. She soon began to manufacture the actual full-scale sets and props for the Park, with her favorite project being the design and construction of the Enchanted Tiki Room birds. The Haunted Mansion Attraction, Pirates of the Caribbean Attraction, "it's a small world," and Storybook Land Canal Boats were some of her other notable projects.

BRUCE BUSHMAN
Disneyland

Bruce Bushman began as an artist in the Studio's story department in 1937. For *Disneyland* Park, Bruce was a principal designer for the Casey Jr. Circus Train and its whimsical station, the Phantom Boats, the cars for Mr. Toad's Wild Ride, the ships for Peter Pan's Flight Attraction, Dumbo the Flying Elephant Attraction, and the teacups for the Mad Tea Party. He also conceived the Monstro the Whale set piece for Fantasyland Area. To preserve the beautiful carvings on King Arthur Carrousel, Bruce designed a high, peaked canopy to fit over the whole machine. He restored the carrousel's horses and converted the ride's original sleighs into train cars for the Casey Jr. Circus Train. Because Bruce was a big, husky fellow, Walt instructed his ride designers to use Bruce's proportions when designing the seats for their attractions.

HANK DAINS
Walt Disney World

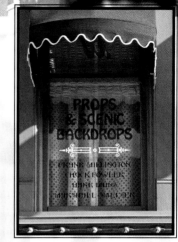

Hank Dains was hired into the Studio's drapery department in June of 1955 before transitioning to *Disneyland* Park in 1964, where he was a key figure in creating the Park's decorating department. His division maintained attraction show scenes and parade floats, decorated the interiors of the Resort hotel rooms, and decked out Main Street, U.S.A. Area in *Disneyland* Park for Christmas. He transferred to *Walt Disney World* Resort after its opening. Dains is legendary for preventing after-hours Christmas disasters. He fixed the Christmas tree in *Disneyland* Park in three days when it was significantly damaged. When the tree in *Walt Disney World* Resort was snapped in half by high winds, he topped his earlier achievement by completely un-decorating the tree, rejoining the two pieces with a metal brace, and re-decorating it in time for the Park's opening the next morning!

CLAUDE COATS *Disneyland and Walt Disney World*

An animation background painter at the Studio since 1935, Claude Coats went to work for WED in 1955. His first assignment was to create the model for Mr. Toad's Wild Ride. He later painted the fluorescent floor-to-ceiling backgrounds in the Fantasyland dark rides and contributed to Pirates of the Caribbean Attraction, The Haunted Mansion Attraction, the Submarine Voyage, and the Grand Canyon and Primeval World dioramas. It was to Claude that, while working on the Rainbow Caverns Mine Train, Walt uttered the famous line "It's kind of fun to do the impossible." For *Walt Disney World* Resort, Claude contributed backgrounds to the Mickey Mouse Revue in Fantasyland Area and created If You Had Wings in Tomorrowland Area. He designed the facade for The Haunted Mansion and acted as art director for the 20,000 Leagues Under the Sea and Snow White's Scary Adventures attractions. He later lent his talents to the Universe of Energy, Horizons, and World of Motion pavilions in *Epcot®*. The "Big and Tall" reference in his *Disneyland* Park window refers to Claude's height. He stood 6'6" tall.

MARC DAVIS

Disneyland and Walt Disney World

One of Walt's legendary "Nine Old Men" of animation, Marc Davis later transitioned to WED to play a key role in designing The Haunted Mansion Attraction, The Enchanted Tiki Room, and "it's a small world" Attraction. His dozens of sketches for Pirates of the Caribbean Attraction, including the famous jail scene, are now legendary as a result of the namesake motion pictures. Marc was the first to add humor to the attractions when he was asked by Walt in 1964 to add comedic touches to the nine-year-old Jungle Cruise Attraction. This changed the attraction from a "True–Life Adventure" to a humorous show, an idea that was controversial at the time. He also created America Sings in Tomorrowland Area. (Upon that attraction's closing, the bulk of its characters became the cast for Splash Mountain Attraction.) For *Walt Disney World* Resort, Marc created Country Bear Jamboree and was art director for Jungle Cruise. He later consulted on the World of Motion pavilion in *Epcot®*. Marc's *Disneyland* Park window makes reference to his extensive collection of New Guinea art.

MARVIN DAVIS *Disneyland and Walt Disney World*

One of WED's master planners, Marvin Davis was responsible for drawing up the initial site plan that became the blueprint for *Disneyland* Park. His drawing, dated September 1953, was the first to contain the "central hub" concept. Marvin also worked on Main Street, U.S.A. Area; Sleeping Beauty Castle; and The Haunted Mansion Attraction in *Disneyland* Park. While it took sixty-nine tries to finalize the master plan for 200 acres of *Disneyland* Park, Marvin was able to lay out the initial 27,000 acres of *Walt Disney World* Resort after only seven attempts. While the Florida site was being planned, Marvin was known to translate Walt's ideas for *Epcot®* from sketches Walt drew on napkins. He closely worked on Disney's Contemporary Resort, Golf Resort (now Shades of Green), and Disney's Polynesian Resort for *Walt Disney World* Resort.

ELIAS DISNEY *Disneyland and Walt Disney World*

Elias Disney, Walt and Roy's father, became a contractor in Chicago in 1895. Starting out as a carpenter, he later built houses that were designed by his wife, Flora. He eventually built a house for his own family at 1249 Tripp Avenue, where Walt was born on December 5, 1901. Elias's window is one of many along Main Street, U.S.A. Area, in *Walt Disney World* Resort honoring Disney family members.

ROY O. DISNEY *Walt Disney World*

In 1923, Roy O. Disney started The Walt Disney Studio with his younger brother, Walt. Roy contributed $250, Walt had $40, and they borrowed $500 from an uncle. With Walt as the creative force of the company, Roy handled the company's finances, once stating, "My job is to help Walt do the things he wants to do." It was Roy who sold the weekly *Disneyland* television show to the ABC network in September of 1953, which gave Walt the funds to build *Disneyland* Park. After Walt's death in 1966, Roy postponed his retirement to personally supervise the planning and construction of the "Disney World" project, which he renamed *Walt Disney World* Resort as a tribute to his brother. His pseudonym, Roy Davis, is also listed on a window. It's the name he used when traveling to Florida when the company secretly acquired the land for *Walt Disney World* Resort in 1964.

WALTER E. DISNEY *Disneyland and Walt Disney World*

One of the creators of Mickey Mouse, creative genius, and co-founder of The Walt Disney Company, Walt Disney would often take his two daughters to ride the local carousel on weekends at Griffith Park in Los Angeles, while he had to sit on a bench and watch. This led him to the idea of creating an amusement enterprise where parents and children "could have fun together." He broke ground for *Disneyland* Park in July of 1954 and opened the Park almost exactly a year later, on July 17, 1955. With the phenomenal success of the California park, Walt began thinking even bigger, eventually acquiring 27,000 acres in central Florida to build his Vacation Kingdom, which became *Walt Disney World* Resort. His name appears on windows in *Walt Disney World* Resort and was added to a window in *Disneyland* Park during the Park's fiftieth anniversary.

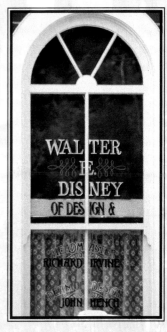

RON DOMINGUEZ *Disneyland*

Ron Dominguez's family home once stood in the Anaheim orange groves that Walt purchased for his Park. (It was situated between what are now the sites of Pirates of the Caribbean Attraction and Café Orleans.) A ticket taker on Opening Day of *Disneyland* Park in 1955, Ron graduated to portraying Davy Crockett in *Disneyland* Park. Not liking the attention that came with being a Frontierland celebrity, Ron traded in his coonskin cap and worked his way up to executive vice president of Walt Disney Attractions, West Coast.

MORGAN "BILL" EVANS

Disneyland and Walt Disney World

Bill Evans was the landscaper for Walt's Holmby Hills home when Walt asked him to landscape *Disneyland* Park. After heading to the proposed site to inspect the existing trees, Bill tagged the ones he wanted to keep with a green ribbon and the ones he didn't want with a red ribbon. Unfortunately, the bulldozer driver was color-blind and leveled everything in sight! Bill also acquired the plans for the early expansion of the Southern California freeway system and grabbed the mature trees about to be bulldozed, relocating them to *Disneyland* Park. For Adventureland Area, he combined tropical plants from all over the world and went so far as to plant orange trees upside down so the gnarled roots would look like exotic jungle branches. Bill was the first Disney builder to move to Florida for the *Walt Disney World* Resort project. He landscaped the entire site and oversaw the relocation of 2,000 trees and the laying of enough sod to cover 500 football fields. He continued as a consultant to all Disney parks through *Disney's Animal Kingdom* Theme Park and advised on tropical horticulture for Hong Kong Disneyland.

BOB FOSTER *Walt Disney World*

In 1964, Bob Foster was working as legal counsel for *Disneyland* Park when he was given the task of acquiring the land for Project X, which was to become *Walt Disney World* Resort. Acting with utmost secrecy to avoid the appearance of having any connection to Disney (and thus drive up land values), Bob used the surname Price (his middle name) during his travels to central Florida. He

used dummy corporations, such as Bay Lake Properties, Ayefour Corporation, and Reedy Creek Ranch, to purchase the land on Walt's behalf. He was initially sent to acquire 5,000 acres, but he would eventually execute forty-seven transactions, purchasing more than 27,000 acres for the company. His "Pseudonym Real Estate Dev. Co." window also lists his "Bob Price" alias.

VAN ARSDALE FRANCE *Disneyland*

Wanting to avoid a carnival image for his new park, Walt hired Van Arsdale France in March of 1955 to create the employee orientation and training programs that eventually became Disney University. Van introduced the idea that new employees would be part of the "show" that was *Disneyland* Park; thus they would be its "Cast Members," and the Park's customers would be their "Guests." He strongly felt that every Guest at *Disneyland* Park deserved the VIP treatment, but he created a less formal backstage workplace atmosphere, stating, "The only Mister here is Mister Toad."

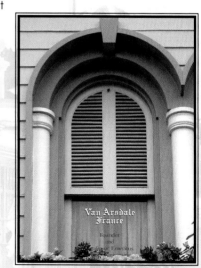

BLAINE GIBSON

*Disneyland and
Walt Disney World*

The winner of a soap-sculpting contest as a child, Blaine Gibson was actually an animator at the Studio when Walt recruited him in 1954 to sculpt for *Disneyland* Park after taking note of the sculptures in Blaine's office. During his career, Blaine created figures for "it's a small world," The Enchanted Tiki Room, The Haunted Mansion Attraction, Country Bear Jamboree Show, and Pirates of the Caribbean Attraction. He sculpted more than half of the presidents for The Hall of Presidents in *Walt Disney World* Resort, coming out of retirement to sculpt Bill Clinton and George W. Bush. He also created Ben Franklin, Mark Twain, and Will Rogers for The American Adventure in *Epcot*®, and John Wayne and James Cagney for The Great Movie Ride in *Disney's Hollywood Studios*. He later sculpted the Walt and Mickey Mouse "Partners" statue that graces each *Magic Kingdom* central plaza.

BOB GURR

Disneyland and Walt Disney World

Bob Gurr's first brush with Disney was as Disney Legend Ub Iwerks's paperboy. Hired in 1954 to work at Roger Broggie's Studio machine shop, Bob designed the cars for the Autopia Attraction in *Disneyland* Park as his first task. He would go on to develop more than 100 designs for Disney attractions, including the Matterhorn Bobsleds; the *Disneyland* Park and *Walt Disney World* Resort monorails; the antique cars, double-decker buses, and fire engine of Main Street, U.S.A. Area; the *Disneyland* Flying Saucers and Viewliner train; the *Disneyland* Railroad cars; and the parking lot trams; and the Doom Buggies of The Haunted Mansion Attraction. He was also responsible for the initial drawing and plans for the Disneyland Submarine Voyage, and he played a key role in the development of the *Audio-Animatronics* Figure of Abraham Lincoln. The Meteor Cycle Co. heading in his Disneyland window references Bob's love of mountain biking.

YALE GRACEY *Walt Disney World*

A mechanical genius and tinkerer, Yale Gracey was a layout artist at the Studio before 1961, when he moved over to WED to become a special-effects and lighting artist. He is best known for his elaborate effects in The Haunted Mansion Attraction. Together with Imagineer Rolly Crump, he created the entire attraction's unique effects, including the séance room and the graveyard scene's singing busts. He made use of the "Pepper's Ghost" reflection technique, which plays a prominent role in the attraction's ballroom scene and hitchhiking-ghost ending. Yale also invented and installed the fire effect in the "burning town" scene in Pirates of the Caribbean Attraction.

JOHN HENCH *Disneyland and Walt Disney World*

John Hench was a sketch artist at the Studio before transferring to WED in 1954. His initial work was on Tomorrowland Area, but he moved on to design Adventureland buildings and walkways, New Orleans Square, Snow White Grotto, and the Park's costumed characters. John was Imagineering's color expert, famous for using twenty-five shades of white on the Ford Pavilion for the 1964–1965 New York World's Fair. Later, he was a key figure in the designing and planning of *Walt Disney World* Resort, where he adjusted the entire Resort's color palette to work better with the direct Florida sun. Some of the most renowned facilities in the Disney parks were designed by John, including Spaceship Earth for *Epcot®* and the iconic Space Mountain Attraction. Walt appointed John as Mickey Mouse's official portrait artist. John's first portrait, for which he was paid $150, was for Mickey's twenty-fifth birthday. He worked for the company until the age of ninety-five, once stating, "There's no trick to it. You just have to love your work."

RICHARD IRVINE

Disneyland and Walt Disney World

A set designer with a degree in architecture, Richard "Dick" Irvine joined the Studio in 1942 and was chosen by Walt in 1953 to act as a liaison with the outside architectural firms hired to design *Disneyland* Park. He recruited motion-picture art directors Marvin Davis and Bill Martin to assist in developing preliminary concepts for Walt's proposed park. Supervising artists, architects, engineers, and designers, Dick was Walt's key conduit to the creative team of Imagineers. He also oversaw the planning and designing of *Walt Disney World* Resort as WED's vice president of design.

ROBERT F. JANI
Disneyland and Walt Disney World

Initially the head of the *Disneyland* Park Guest Relations department from 1955 to 1957, Bob Jani left the company for ten years, to return in 1967 as director of entertainment. He eventually became vice president of entertainment for *Disneyland* Park and *Walt Disney World* Resort. For *Walt Disney World* Resort, he oversaw the Resort's opening events and created the Electrical Water Pageant. Bob's most notable achievement was the Main Street Electrical Parade, which he conceived as a morale booster for *Disneyland* Park Cast Members after the opening of *Walt Disney World* Resort.

FRED JOERGER *Disneyland and Walt Disney World*

Fred Joerger was hired in 1953 as a model builder, with his first *Disneyland* Park model being the *Mark Twain* steamboat. He became the company's resident "rock expert," designing all the rockwork and waterfalls for Jungle Cruise Attraction and Swiss Family Treehouse in *Walt Disney World* Resort, and the atrium waterfall and the original swimming pool for Disney's Polynesian Resort. For both *Disneyland* Park and *Walt Disney World* Resort, Fred created the rocky facades for Big Thunder Mountain Railroad Attraction. He also contributed to The Haunted Mansion Attraction, Pirates of the Caribbean Attraction, and Tom Sawyer Island. The "Daughterland Modeling Agency" heading in his *Walt Disney World* Resort window refers to the fact that the WED model shop was populated with many daughters of WED and Disney executives during the 1960s, especially during school summer vacation.

BILL JUSTICE *Disneyland and Walt Disney World*

An expert at programming *Audio-Animatronics* Figures, Bill Justice started as an animator for the Studio in 1937. His artistic talent can be seen in the Sleeping Beauty paintings in the King Arthur Carrousel in *Disneyland* Park. In 1965 he went to work for WED, where his first assignment was programming the *Audio-Animatronics* Figures for Pirates of the Caribbean Attraction. For *Walt Disney World* Resort, Bill was art director for Peter Pan's Flight Attraction in Fantasyland Area and programmed the figures for The Hall of Presidents, Country Bear Jamboree Show, and The Mickey Mouse Revue, which he also conceived. Bill designed the floats and costumes for the *Disneyland* Park Christmas parade in 1959, and he also made the initial sketches for the Main Street Electrical Parade.

JACK LINDQUIST

Disneyland and Walt Disney World

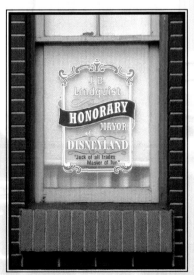

Jack Lindquist was working for a Los Angeles advertising firm when *Disneyland* Park officials contacted him to ask if he could recommend an advertising person for the Park. Jack recommended himself, becoming the Park's first advertising manager in 1955. He was instrumental in the creation of the Magic Kingdom Club, the Ambassador Program, Disney Dollars, Disney's Grad Nites, the Park's New Year's Eve celebrations, and the *Disneyland* Park tenth birthday celebration, which he named "Tencennial." He was marketing director for the opening of *Walt Disney World* Resort and was later named *Disneyland* Park president. The "Peterson Travel Agency" heading in his *Walt Disney World* Resort window refers to his family's original surname of Peterson—the family thought it was too common when they arrived in America and changed it to Lindquist.

BOB MATHEISON
Walt Disney World (two windows)

A former *Walt Disney World* Resort executive vice president, Parks, Bob Matheison started at *Disneyland* Park in 1960 as a sound coordinator, teaching Jungle Cruise guides to talk into microphones and ticket takers to talk to the Guests. He became manager of Guest Relations and talent manager of *Disneyland* Park before being picked by Walt to head the Disney contingent for the 1964–1965 New York World's Fair. After the fair, Bob spent three years as part of a small WED group called Project Development that compiled research and made recommendations to Walt and the other designers working on the Florida project. In 1970 he was named director of operations for *Walt Disney World* Resort, where he helped develop the Resort's operating plan.

SAM MCKIM
Disneyland and Walt Disney World

Sam McKim was hired as an illustrator for WED Enterprises in 1954. Dubbed the "quintessential researcher" by Marty Sklar, Sam created historically accurate drawings that were known for their fine detail. His first *Disneyland* Park sketches were for the Golden Horseshoe Revue and the shops, restaurants, and attractions in Frontierland Area and on Main Street, U.S.A. Area. His many attraction-concept contributions include Great Moments with Mr. Lincoln, Walt Disney's Carousel of Progress, Pirates of the Caribbean Attraction, The Haunted Mansion Attraction, The Hall of Presidents, the Universe of Energy in *Epcot*®, and The Great Movie Ride, among others, in *Disney's Hollywood Studios*. Sam also drew the first *Disneyland* Park map that was sold to Guests, which he updated as Walt added attractions.

EDWARD T. MECK
Disneyland

Eddie Meck was the first publicity chief for *Disneyland* Park, hired five months before the Park opened in 1955. Already a seasoned entertainment publicist, he feared the press would think his *Disneyland* Park press releases were hype. He decided to give them firsthand exposure and invited them for Opening Day of the Park, thus inventing the "press invited" opening that would become a tradition for Disney Parks. Eddie later assisted with the opening of *Walt Disney World* Resort.

TOM NABBE *Walt Disney World*

The "Sawyer's Fence Painting Co." heading in Tom Nabbe's *Walt Disney World* Resort window actually references his *Disneyland* Park career. Tom was handpicked to portray Tom Sawyer on Tom Sawyer Island by Walt himself, who said he "looked the part." To keep the job, Walt required Tom to maintain a C average in school, and he had to take his report card directly to Walt every quarter for inspection. After his stint as Tom Sawyer, he went on to manage other *Disneyland* Park attractions before transferring to *Walt Disney World* Resort in 1971 as monorail manager. Tom retired as manager of Distribution Services after a forty-eight-year Disney career and holds the distinction of being the last working member of Club 55, the group of *Disneyland* Park Cast Members who started their careers during the Park's opening year.

DICK NUNIS *Disneyland and Walt Disney World*

The former chairman of Walt Disney Attractions, Dick Nunis was hired by Van Arsdale France in May of 1955 as an orientation training instructor for $1.80 an hour (though he claims Van promised him $2). He quickly rose through the managerial ranks, becoming director of Park Operations in 1961. That same year, he started consulting on "Project X," which was to become *Walt Disney World* Resort. In 1971, he was named executive vice president of *Walt Disney World* Resort and *Disneyland* Park. As chairman of the Parks and Resorts division, Dick was the operations chief for Disney's expansion into Japan and France. The "Wave Machines a Specialty" line on his *Disneyland* Park window refers to a wave machine Dick had installed in Seven Seas Lagoon in *Walt Disney World* Resort. The machine was quickly removed because it was causing erosion of the lagoon's islands.

OWEN POPE *Walt Disney World*

The original horse trainer for the Disney parks, Owen Pope holds the distinction of having lived on the Studio lot in Burbank, in *Disneyland* Park, and in *Walt Disney World* Resort. After catching Owen's Shetland pony horse show in November 1951, Walt invited Owen and his wife, Dolly, to move the whole enterprise to the Studio lot, where they constructed stables and lived in their trailer under the Studio's water tower for the next two and a half years. Acquiring and training the horses for the Anaheim park, as well as building the saddles, coaches, and wagons for Frontierland Area, Owen and Dolly moved to *Disneyland* Park three days before its opening, becoming the Park's only residents. They relocated once more in January 1971, to *Walt Disney World* Resort, where Owen was the manager for the opening of the Tri-Circle D Ranch at Disney's Fort Wilderness Resort & Campground.

JOE POTTER *Walt Disney World*

General William E. "Joe" Potter was executive vice president of the 1964–1965 New York World's Fair when he was hired by Walt in 1965 to work on his secret Florida project. While Admiral Joe Fowler was responsible for *Magic Kingdom* Park in Florida, Joe Potter was in charge of the governmental aspects and infrastructure of the property. His team moved over seven million cubic yards of dirt for *Magic Kingdom* Park and dug more than fifty-five miles of water-drainage canals. He built the underground Utilidor system, supervised building design, and created innovative sewage, power, and water-treatment plants. His window's heading, "General Joe's Building Permits," makes reference to his division's governmental responsibility to review and approve all building structure plans during the construction of *Walt Disney World* Resort.

WATHEL ROGERS *Disneyland and Walt Disney World*

Wathel Rogers was a founding member of WED's model shop in 1954, having started with the company in 1939 as an animator. His two-week WED assignment to build architectural models for *Disneyland* Park turned into a career that saw him become a pioneer in research and development at Imagineering. Wathel was known as Mr. *Audio-Animatronics*, and his many projects included The Enchanted Tiki Room, Walt Disney's Carousel of Progress, Pirates of the Caribbean Attraction, Great Moments with Mr. Lincoln, Jungle Cruise Attraction, America Sings, and The American Adventure in *Epcot*®. He later served as the art director for *Magic Kingdom* Park in *Walt Disney World* Resort after its opening in 1971.

HERB RYMAN

Disneyland and Walt Disney World

Over two stressful days in September of 1953 known as the "lost-weekend," Herbert Dickens Ryman drew the first sketch of what would be *Disneyland* Park. Roy Disney needed it that Monday morning for a presentation on the Park to potential investors. Herb sketched as Walt stood by his side describing his vision of the Park. During his career, Herb illustrated concepts for New Orleans Square, Pirates of the Caribbean Attraction, Jungle Cruise Attraction, and both *Disneyland* Park and *Walt Disney World* Resort castles. For *Walt Disney World* Resort, Herb helped develop The Hall of Presidents and played a key role in conceptualizing the American Adventure and China pavilions in *Epcot*®. He also illustrated numerous concepts for the entire Park.

MARTY SKLAR *Walt Disney World*

The former president and vice-chairman and principal creative executive of Walt Disney Imagineering, Marty Sklar began his Disney career a month before *Disneyland* Park opened, while still a twenty-one-year-old student at UCLA. He created the *Disneyland News,* an 1890s-style souvenir newspaper, and was soon responsible for writing most of the *Disneyland* Park marketing materials and souvenir pictorials. Starting in the late 1950s, Marty was Walt's personal writer and served as lead communicator of Walt's concepts for *Walt Disney World* Resort and *Epcot®.* Marty also wrote Walt's messages for the company's annual reports. He joined WED in 1961, where he later wrote the scripts for Walt's announcement of *Walt Disney World* Resort and for the film in which Walt described his vision for *Epcot®.* Marty became Imagineering's creative leader in 1974 and was named Imagineering Ambassador in 2006.

BILL SULLIVAN

Walt Disney World (two windows)

Bill "Sully" Sullivan began his career in *Disneyland* Park in 1955 as a ticket taker on Jungle Cruise Attraction. He became a ride operator, then a *Disneyland* Park operations supervisor before working with Bob

Matheison and Bob Allen on the Project Management team for *Walt Disney World* Resort in 1968. After moving to Florida, Bill was responsible for Main Street, U.S.A. Area; Adventureland Area; and Liberty Square on Opening Day of *Magic Kingdom* Park in *Walt Disney World* Resort, and eventually became the Park's vice president. "Sully's Safaris" alludes to Bill's love of hunting and fishing.

DONN TATUM

Walt Disney World

Donn Tatum was West Coast vice president of the ABC Television Network in 1953 when he sat in on the infamous meeting during which Roy O. Disney pitched the idea of *Disneyland* Park to the network. Donn was enthusiastic about the project from the start, so much so that he became

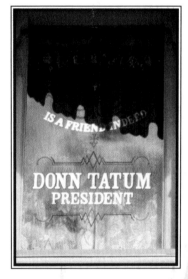

production business manager at the Studio in 1956. He rose to become executive vice president of *Disneyland* Park and later was called on to assist with the Florida land acquisition for *Walt Disney World* Resort. He played a major role in the Resort's creation, and he was named the first president of *Walt Disney World* Resort. Donn succeeded Roy Disney as chief executive officer and chairman of the board for Walt Disney Productions in 1971, becoming the first non–Disney family member to hold those titles.

CARD WALKER

Walt Disney World

E. Cardon Walker started in the Studio mailroom in 1938 and later held positions in marketing, operations, and advertising, and he was also involved in the Florida land acquisition for *Walt Disney World* Resort. Named company president in 1971 and later becoming CEO in 1976, he was the leader in taking *Epcot*® from dream to reality. The "Licensed Practitioner of Psychiatry and Justice of the Peace" mention in his window refers to a CEO's need to have psychiatric powers to keep his organization's diverse talents moving in the same direction, ensuring that "justice" is done and "peace" is maintained.

ROBERT "BUD" WASHO

Disneyland and Walt Disney World

Bud Washo was hired in 1954 as the superintendent of the Staff and Plaster shop for *Disneyland* Park. He and his crew were responsible for the molding, casting, and finishing of a vast array of unique Disney Park elements, including Autopia cars, Jungle Cruise elephants, Primeval World dinosaurs, fiberglass stone archways, plaster rock battlements, and golden castle turrets. To create the mountain for Matterhorn Bobsleds, Bud and his team laid four acres of plaster. In Orlando, he used an old fertilizer storage shed as the initial workshop for molding and creating the components for Cinderella Castle in *Walt Disney World* Resort. He later became Architectural Ornamentation manager for World Showcase in *Epcot*®, where he enhanced and maintained the old, authentic look of the pavilions using modern materials.

FRANK G. WELLS

Disneyland and Walt Disney World

An avid adventurer, Frank G. Wells was president of The Walt Disney Company from 1984 until 1994. During his tenure, Frank was instrumental in the renaissance of the Disney theme parks with the building of Disney-MGM Studios (now *Disney's Hollywood Studios*); Euro Disneyland (now *Disneyland Resort Paris*); various Disney water parks, hotels, and resort districts; and attraction additions and upgrades to existing parks. The "Seven Summits" mention in his window refers to Frank's 1986 book, *Seven Summits,* which detailed his adventures climbing the highest mountain on each of the seven continents. In the Matterhorn Bobsleds Attraction in *Disneyland* Park, one can spot a "Wells Expedition" crate in his honor. In *Walt Disney World* Resort, his window is one of only two third-floor windows in Main Street, U.S.A. Area, a tribute to his quest to reach the highest peaks in the world.

Disneyland

Walt Disney World

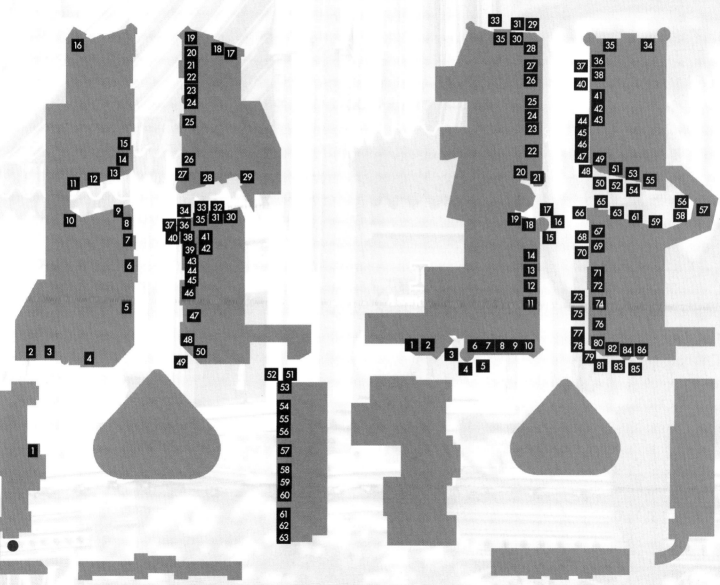

WINDOWS BY NUMBER

DISNEYLAND

Casting Agency Door	DISNEY, WALTER E.
1	LINDQUIST, JACK
2	BURNS, HARRIET
3	BOYER, CHARLES
4	COATS, CLAUDE
5	DISNEY, ELIAS
6	ROGERS, WATHEL
7	MANG, M. A.
8	ALLEN, W. F.
8	PATTERSON, C. V.
9	GILMORE, D. S.
9	UPJOHN, E. G.
10	MILLER, CHRISTOPHER D.
11	JOERGER, FRED
12	WINGER, ED
13	CONLEY, RENIE
14	CLARK, ROYAL
15	BOAG, WALLY
16	PENFIELD, BOB
17	IRVINE, ALEXANDER R.
18	ELLENSHAW, PETER
18	HENCH, JOHN
18	RYMAN, HERB
19	McKIM, SAM
20	BARDEAU, RENIE
21	RIGDON, CICELY
22	MECK, EDWARD T.
23	CRUMP, ROLLY
24	EDGREN, DON
25	BRIGHT, C. RANDY
26	BARNARD, H. DRAEGART
27	CORA, JIM
28	GURR, BOB
29	JUSTICE, BILL
30	COTTRELL, W. DENNIS
31	FERRANTE, ORLANDO
32	SHOCKEY, CASH
32	MARTIN, IVAN
32	ROREX, JACK
33	WASHO, ROBERT "BUD"
34	MOREY, SEB
35	WHITNEY, GEORGE
36	BOYAJIAN, CHUCK
37	KURI, EMILE
38	ALEXANDER, CHARLES
38	CONWAY, RAY
38	MILLS, GEORGE
39	ROTH, L. H.
40	DOMINGUEZ, RON
41	BUSHMAN, BRUCE
41	DAGRADI, DON
42	ANDERSON, KEN
43	LEOPOLD, FREDERIC
43	YOUNGMAN, GORDON
44	LESSING, GUNTHER R.
45	DAVIS, MARC
46	EMMER, GREG
47	FRANCE, VAN ARSDALE
48	BROGGIE, ROGER
49	AMEMIYA, HIDEO
50	NUNIS, DICK
51	CATONE, JOHN LOUIS
52	VAN DE WARKER, RAY
53	ATENCIO, X
54	ALBRIGHT, MILT
55	GIBSON, BLAINE
56	EVANS, MORGAN "BILL"
57	JANI, ROBERT F.
58	PATRICK, GEORGE
58	RUBOTTOM, WADE B.
59	MARTIN, WILSON "BILL"
59	SCOGNAMILLO, GABRIEL
60	DAVIS, MARVIN
60	IRVINE, RICHARD
61	WELLS, FRANK G.
62	HAMEL, J. S.
63	WHEELER, WILLIAM T.
63	WISE, JOHN

WALT DISNEY WORLD

Train Station, Casting Agency Door at Disney Clothiers, 154	DISNEY, WALTER E.
1	BROGGIE, ROGER
2	POPE, OWEN
3	BAKER, BUDDY
4	JACKMAN, BOB
5	BRUNS, GEORGE
6	LOGAN, RON
7	LINDLEY, LONNIE
8	BULLARD, ED
9	JANI, ROBERT F.
10	CORSON, CHARLES
11	KURI, EMILE
12	RIDGWAY, CHARLIE
13	CARLSON, JOYCE
14	BOOTH, BOB
14	BROGGIE, ROGER JR.
14	FRANKIE, JOHN
14	GALLAGHER, NEIL
14	GLADISH, JACK
14	PENA, RUDY
14	SCHWENINGER, DAVE
14	VAN EVERY, DICK
14	VERITY, JIM
15	HOUSER, MORRIE
15	JENNINGS, LOU
15	JOYCE, JOHN
16	EDGREN, DON
16	WISE, JOHN
17	KLUG, KEN
17	MASLAK, STAN
17	ZOVICH, JOHN
18	SNYDER, DAVID
18, 50	BAGNALL, MICHAEL
19	WALSH, BILL
20	ROBINSON, CECIL
21	LINDQUIST, JACK
22	GENGENBACH, DAVE
22	GURR, BOB
22	McGINNIS, GEORGE
22	WATKINS, BILL
23	VILMER, EARL
24	WALKER, CARD
25	CROWELL, TED
25	LINDBERG, ARNOLD
26	COATS, CLAUDE
26	DAVIS, MARC
27	DeCUIR, JOHN
27	JUSTICE, BILL
28	ARMSTRONG, JIM
29	CURRY, JOHN
30	ROLAND, HOWARD
31	GARVES, STAN

32	BAXTER, TONY
32	BURKHART, DAVE
32	JOHNSON, ED
32	YOUNGER, GARY
33	KENT, RALPH
34	SLOCUM, LARRY
35	BRUMMITT, HOWARD
35	DAVIS, MARVIN
35	GREEN, VIC
35	HENCH, JOHN
35	HOPE, FRED
35	IRVINE, RICHARD
35	MARTIN, WILSON "BILL"
35	MYALL, CHUCK
36, 54	SULLIVAN, BILL
37, 54	MATHEISON, BOB
38	MILLER, CHRISTOPHER D.
38	MILLER, JENNIFER
38	MILLER, JOANNA
38	MILLER, PATRICK
38	MILLER, RON and DIANE
38	MILLER, RONALD JR.
38	MILLER, TAMARA
38	MILLER, WALTER
39	IWERKS, DON
39	IWERKS, UB
40	WASHO, BILL
40	WASHO, ROBERT "BUD"
41	NUNIS, DICK
42	MILLER, RON
43	FERRANTE, ORLANDO
44	DISNEY, ABIGAIL
44	DISNEY, ROY PATRICK
45	DISNEY, PATTY
45	DISNEY, ROY E.
46	DISNEY, SUSAN
46	DISNEY, TIMOTHY
47	EVANS, MORGAN "BILL"
47	VIRGINIA, TONY
48	TATUM, DONN
49	WELLS, FRANK G.
50	BONGIRNO, CARL
50	McMANUS, JIM
50	ROBERTSON, WARREN
50	TRYON, LARRY
51	McCLURE, NEAL
51	MORROW, DICK
51	OLIN, SPENCE
51	ROSS, JIM
51	SMITH, PHIL
52	DYER, BONAR
53	DAINS, HANK
53	FOWLER, CHUCK
53	MILLINGTON, FRANK
53	SMELSER, MARSHALL
54	SULLIVAN, BILL
54	MATHEISON, BOB
54	ALLEN, BOB
54	CRIMMINGS, PETE
54	EVANS, DICK
54	HOELSCHER, BILL
55	OLSEN, JACK
56	CLARK, PETE
57	SAYERS, JACK
58	FAGRELL, NORM
59	DARE, BUD
60	BLAIR, MARY
60	CAMPBELL, COLLIN
60	GIBSON, BLAINE
60	REDMOND, DOROTHEA
60	RYMAN, HERB
61	BROWNING, NOLAN
62	DISNEY, ROY U. (listed as Roy Davis)
62	FOSTER, BOB (listed as Bob Price)
63	DISNEY, ELIAS
64	CHAPMAN, KEN
64	HARTLEY, PAUL
64	McKIM, SAM
64	PLUMMER, ELMER
64	PRINZHORN, ERNIE
65	JEFFERDS, VINCE
66	TONARELY, LOU
66	WATT, WILBUR K.
67	LUND, BRADFORD
67	LUND, MICHELLE
67	LUND, VICTORIA
67	LUND, WILLIAM and SHARON
68	COBB, MALCOLM
68	FERGES, JACK
68	JOERGER, FRED
68	NATSUME, MITZ
68	SEWELL, BOB
69	COCKERELL, LEE A.
70	LAVAL, BRUCE
71	EASTMAN, TOM
71	PASSILLA, JAMES
71	VAUGHN, PAT
72	NABBE, TOM
73	GRACEY, YALE
73	MARTIN, BUD
73	O'BRIEN, KEN
73	ROGERS, WATHEL
74	BOSCHE, BILL
74	BOYD, JACK
74	GIBEAUT, BOB
74	PFAHLER, DICK
74	STEWART, McLAREN
75	MOORE, C. ROBERT
75	NOCETI, NORM
76	CHISHOLM, ED
76	WILLIAMS, GORDON
77	ATENCIO, X
77	BERTINO, AL
77	SKLAR, MARTY
78	CAYNE, DOUG
78	KRAMER, JOE
78	WINDRUM, GEORGE
79	BOWMAN, RON
79	DURFLINGER, GLENN
79	HOLMQUIST, DON
79	KLINE, DICK
79	NELSON, GEORGE
80	DISNEY, ROY O.
81	POTTER, JOE
82	IRWIN, BILL
82	REISER, LARRY
83	MARKHAM, PETE
84	DINGMAN, DAN
84	STANEK, FRANCIS
85	PHELPS, BOB
86	CREEKMORE, KEN
86	HARRYMAN, ORPHA
86	KEEHNE, JOHN
86	PASKEVICIUS, ALYJA
86	PEIRCE, TOM

23

WINDOWS BY NAME

DISNEYLAND

ALBRIGHT, MILT 54
ALEXANDER, CHARLES 38
ALLEN, W. F. 8
AMEMIYA, HIDEO 49
ANDERSON, KEN 42
ATENCIO, X 53
BARDEAU, RENIE 20
BARNARD, H. DRAEGART 26
BOAG, WALLY 15
BOYAJIAN, CHUCK 36
BOYER, CHARLES 3
BRIGHT, C. RANDY 25
BROGGIE, ROGER 48
BURNS, HARRIET 2
BUSHMAN, BRUCE 41
CATONE, JOHN LOUIS 51
CLARK, ROYAL 14
COATS, CLAUDE 4
CONLEY, RENIE 13
CONWAY, RAY 38
CORA, JIM 27
COTTRELL, W. DENNIS 30
CRUMP, ROLLY 23
DAGRADI, DON 41
DAVIS, MARC 45
DAVIS, MARVIN 60
DISNEY, ELIAS 5
DISNEY, WALTER E. ...... Casting Agency Door
DOMINGUEZ, RON 40
EDGREN, DON 24
ELLENSHAW, PETER 18
EMMER, GREG 46
EVANS, MORGAN "BILL" 56
FERRANTE, ORLANDO 31
FRANCE, VAN ARSDALE 47
GIBSON, BLAINE 55
GILMORE, D. S. 9
GURR, BOB 28
HAMEL, J. S. 62
HENCH, JOHN 18
IRVINE, ALEXANDER R. 17
IRVINE, RICHARD 60
JANI, ROBERT F. 57
JOERGER, FRED 11

JUSTICE, BILL 29
KURI, EMILE 37
LEOPOLD, FREDERIC 43
LESSING, GUNTHER R. 44
LINDQUIST, JACK 1
MANG, M. A. 7
MARTIN, IVAN 32
MARTIN, WILSON "BILL" 59
McKIM, SAM 19
MECK, EDWARD T. 22
MILLER, CHRISTOPHER D. 10
MILLS, GEORGE 38
MOREY, SEB 34
NUNIS, DICK 50
PATRICK, GEORGE 58
PATTERSON, C. V. 8
PENFIELD, BOB 16
RIGDON, CICELY 21
ROGERS, WATHEL 6
ROREX, JACK 32
ROTH, L. H. 39
RUBOTTOM, WADE B. 58
RYMAN, HERB 18
SCOGNAMILLO, GABRIEL 59
SHOCKEY, CASH 32
UPJOHN, E. G. 9
VAN DE WARKER, RAY 52
WASHO, ROBERT "BUD" 33
WELLS, FRANK G. 61
WHEELER, WILLIAM T. 63
WHITNEY, GEORGE 35
WINGER, ED 12
WISE, JOHN 63
YOUNGMAN, GORDON 43

WALT DISNEY WORLD

ALLEN, BOB 54
ARMSTRONG, JIM 28
ATENCIO, X 77
BAGNALL, MICHAEL 18, 50
BAKER, BUDDY 3
BAXTER, TONY 32
BERTINO, AL 77
BLAIR, MARY 60

BONGIRNO, CARL 50
BOOTH, BOB 14
BOSCHE, BILL 74
BOWMAN, RON 79
BOYD, JACK 74
BROGGIE, ROGER 1
BROGGIE, ROGER JR. 14
BROWNING, NOLAN 61
BRUMMITT, HOWARD 35
BRUNS, GEORGE 5
BULLARD, ED 8
BURKHART, DAVE 32
CAMPBELL, COLLIN 60
CARLSON, JOYCE 13
CAYNE, DOUG 78
CHAPMAN, KEN 64
CHISHOLM, ED 76
CLARK, PETE 56
COATS, CLAUDE 26
COBB, MALCOLM 68
COCKERELL, LEE A. 69
CORSON, CHARLES 10
CREEKMORE, KEN 86
CRIMMINGS, PETE 54
CROWELL, TED 25
CURRY, JOHN 29
DAINS, HANK 53
DARE, BUD 59
DAVIS, MARC 26
DAVIS, MARVIN 35
DeCUIR, JOHN 27
DINGMAN, DAN 84
DISNEY, ABIGAIL 44
DISNEY, ELIAS 63
DISNEY, PATTY 45
DISNEY, ROY E. 45
DISNEY, ROY O. 80
DISNEY, ROY O.
   (also listed as Roy Davis) 62
DISNEY, ROY PATRICK 44
DISNEY, SUSAN 46
DISNEY, TIMOTHY 46
DISNEY, WALTER E. .... Train Station, Casting
                              Agency Door, 154
DURFLINGER, GLENN 79
DYER, BONAR 52

EASTMAN, TOM......71
EDGREN, DON 16
EVANS, DICK 54
EVANS, MORGAN "BILL"......47
FAGRELL, NORM 58
FERGES, JACK 68
FERRANTE, ORLANDO...... 43
FOSTER, BOB (also listed as Bob Price)......62
FOWLER, CHUCK 53
FRANKIE, JOHN......14
GALLAGHER, NEIL 14
GARVES, STAN 31
GENGENBACH, DAVE 22
GIBEAUT, BOB......74
GIBSON, BLAINE 60
GLADISH, JACK 14
GRACEY, YALE 73
GREEN, VIC 35
GURR, BOB 22
HARRYMAN, ORPHA 86
HARTLEY, PAUL 64
HENCH, JOHN 35
HOELSCHER, BILL 54
HOLMQUIST, DON 79
HOPE, FRED 35
HOUSER, MORRIE 15
IRVINE, RICHARD 35
IRWIN, BILL 82
IWERKS, DON 39
IWERKS, UB 39
JACKMAN, BOB 4
JANI, ROBERT F. 9
JEFFERDS, VINCE 65
JENNINGS, LOU 15
JOERGER, FRED 68
JOHNSON, ED 32
JOYCE, JOHN 15
JUSTICE, BILL 27
KEEHNE, JOHN 86
KENT, RALPH 33
KLINE, DICK 79
KLUG, KEN 17
KRAMER, JOE 78
KURI, EMILE 11
LAVAL, BRUCE...... 70
LINDBERG, ARNOLD 25

LINDLEY, LONNIE 7
LINDQUIST, JACK 21
LOGAN, RON 6
LUND, BRADFORD 67
LUND, MICHELLE...... 67
LUND, VICTORIA...... 67
LUND, WILLIAM and SHARON 67
MARKHAM, PETE 83
MARTIN, BUD 73
MARTIN, WILSON "BILL" 35
MASLAK, STAN 17
MATHEISON, BOB 37, 54
McCLURE, NEAL 51
McGINNIS, GEORGE 22
McKIM, SAM 64
McMANUS, JIM 50
MILLER, CHRISTOPHER D.......38
MILLER, JENNIFER......38
MILLER, JOANNA......38
MILLER, PATRICK......38
MILLER, RON 42
MILLER, RON and DIANE......38
MILLER, RONALD JR.......38
MILLER, TAMARA......38
MILLER, WALTER 38
MILLINGTON, FRANK 53
MOORE, C. ROBERT 75
MORROW, DICK 51
MYALL, CHUCK...... 35
NABBE, TOM 72
NATSUME, MITZ 68
NELSON, GEORGE 79
NOCETI, NORM 75
NUNIS, DICK 41
O'BRIEN, KEN 73
OLIN, SPENCE 51
OLSEN, JACK...... 55
PASKEVICIUS, ALYJA 86
PASILLA, JAMES 71
PEIRCE, TOM 86
PENA, RUDY 14
PFAHLER, DICK 74
PHELPS, BOB 85
PLUMMER, ELMER 64
POPE, OWEN 2
POTTER, JOE......81

PRINZHORN, ERNIE...... 64
REDMOND, DOROTHEA 60
REISER, LARRY 82
RIDGWAY, CHARLIE 12
ROBERTSON, WARREN 50
ROBINSON, CECIL...... 20
ROGERS, WATHEL...... 73
ROLAND, HOWARD 30
ROSS, JIM 51
RYMAN, HERB 60
SAYERS, JACK 57
SCHWENINGER, DAVE 14
SEWELL, BOB 68
SKLAR, MARTY 77
SLOCUM, LARRY 34
SMELSER, MARSHALL 53
SMITH, PHIL 51
SNYDER, DAVID 18
STANEK, FRANCIS...... 84
STEWART, McLAREN 74
SULLIVAN, BILL 36, 54
TATUM, DONN...... 48
TONARELY, LOU 66
TRYON, LARRY 50
VAN EVERY, DICK 15
VAUGHN, PAT 71
VERITY, JIM 14
VILMER, EARL 23
VIRGINIA, TONY......47
WALKER, CARD 24
WALSH, BILL 19
WASHO, BILL 40
WASHO, ROBERT "BUD"...... 40
WATKINS, BILL 22
WATT, WILBUR K. 66
WELLS, FRANK G. 49
WILLIAMS, GORDON 76
WINDRUM, GEORGE...... 78
WISE, JOHN 16
YOUNGER, GARY 32
ZOVICH, JOHN 17

25

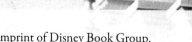

To my "royal" wife, Tracy, and my daughters, Reagan and Brynna. And to my parents, who took me to *Walt Disney World* Resort as a child.

Special thanks to Dave Smith, Robert Tieman, and Ed Ovalle at the Walt Disney Archives, and to Marty Sklar, Dick Nunis, Jack Lindquist, Ron Dominguez, Bob Gurr, Tom Fitzgerald, Bob Matheison, Bill Sullivan, Blaine Gibson, Alex Caruthers, David Golbeck, Alex Wright, and Tony Baxter for their assistance and park anecdotes.

Additional sources used were: *Club 55*, a book dedicated to Disneyland Park original cast members; *Walt Disney's Railroad Story* by Michael Broggie; *Justice for Disney* by Bill Justice; *Designing Disney's Theme Parks* by Karal Ann Marling, Neil Harris, Erika Doss, Yi-Fu Tuan, and Greil Marcus; *Building a Company: Roy O. Disney and the Creation of an Entertainment Empire* by Bob Thomas; *Spinning Disney's World* by Charles Ridgway; *Disneyland: Inside Story* by C. Randy Bright; *Walt Disney Imagineering: A Behind the Dreams Look at Making the Magic Real* by the Imagineers; *The Haunted Mansion: From the Magic Kingdom to the Movies* and *Pirates of the Caribbean: From the Magic Kingdom to the Movies* by Jason Surrell; and *Window on Main Street* by Van Arsdale France.

For information address Disney Editions, 114 Fifth Avenue, New York, New York 10011-5690.
Editorial Director: Wendy Lefkon
Senior Editor: Jody Revenson
Assistant Editor: Jessica Ward
Senior Designer: Tim Palin

ISBN 978-1-4231-0671-5
Library of Congress Cataloging-in-Publication Data on file
Printed in the United States of America
First Edition

The Official Community for Disney Fans
Disney.com/D23